# THE HOUND
## OF THE
# BASKERVILLES

# Dorling  Kindersley

## LONDON, NEW YORK, SYDNEY, DELHI, PARIS, MUNICH and JOHANNESBURG

**Produced by Leapfrog Press Ltd**

**Editor** Zahavit Shalev
**Art Editor** Adrienne Hutchinson
**For Dorling Kindersley**
**Senior Editor** Alastair Dougall
**Managing Art Editor** Jacquie Gulliver
**Picture Research** Liz Moore
**Production** Jo Rooke
**Abridgement** Marie Greenwood

First American Edition, 2000

00 01 02 04 05 10 9 8 7 6 5 4 3 2 1

Published in the United States by Dorling Kindersley Publishing, Inc.
95 Madison Avenue, New York, New York 10016

Dorling Kindersley books are available at special discounts for bulk purchases for sales promotions or premiums. Special editions, including personalized covers, excerpts of existing guides, and corporate imprints can be created in large quantities for specific needs. For more information, contact Special Markets Dept., Dorling Kindersley Publishing, Inc., 95 Madison Avenue, New York, NY 10016, Fax: 800-600-9098.

Greenwood, Marie
  The hound of the Baskervilles / by Sir Arthur Conan Doyle ; adapted by Marie Greenwood.—1st American ed.
     P.cm. – (Dorling Kindersley classics)
  Summary: Sherlock Holmes and Dr Watson travel to the bleak wastes of Dartmoor to solve the mystery surrounding the late Sir Charles Baskerville and a ghostly hound. Illustrated notes throughout the text explain the historical background to the story.
     ISBN 0-7894-6108-0
     [1. Mystery and detective stories.] I. Doyle, Arthur Conan, Sir, 1859-1930. Hound of the Baskervilles. II. Title. III. Series.

     PZ7.G85323 Ho 2000
     {Fic] –dc21

99-055204

Color reproduction by Bright Arts, Hong Kong

Printed by Dai Nippon, China

see our complete catalog at
**www.dk.com**

1001400046I979

DORLING KINDERSLEY CLASSICS

# THE HOUND
## OF THE
# BASKERVILLES

### SIR ARTHUR CONAN DOYLE

*Illustrated by*
MARK OLDROYD

A Dorling Kindersley Book

# CONTENTS

*Sherlock Holmes*

*Dr. Watson*

*Barrymore*

*Mrs. Barrymore*

*Beryl Stapleton*

*Mr. Stapleton*

*Laura Lyons*

*Henry Baskerville*

# INTRODUCTION

From the moment the character of Sherlock Holmes first appeared, in the novel "A Study in Scarlet" in 1887, the public was captivated. Six years, and many Holmes adventures later, his creator, Sir Arthur Conan Doyle, tried to "kill off" the famous detective so that he could concentrate on other books, but gave in to popular demand for yet another story. And so *The Hound of the Baskervilles* was published. It proved to be one of the tensest and most sensational of the whole series, with its tale of a family haunted by a terrifying hound from Hell.

This Dorling Kindersley Classic edition, abridged for young readers, brings the setting of the story to life, evoking the bustle of Victorian London, the clutter of Holmes' study, and the eerie, haunted gloom of Dartmoor. Against this compelling backdrop blazes the formidable intelligence of the greatest of all fictional detectives, the unforgettable Sherlock Holmes.

# THE ART OF DETECTION

Sherlock Holmes satisfies a natural human desire to see criminals brought to justice. He is a modern hero because he relies on scientific methods of observation and deduction, and not magic, to right wrongs. By noting tiny details he can reveal a person's past life, his temperament and tastes to the wonderment of others, his only tool a humble magnifying glass. Modern detectives still need to use their wits and intuition, but they also have a host of technological aids to help them in the never-ending war against crime.

## The bad old days

In medieval times, the difficulty of proving a person's guilt led to all kinds of cruel and foolish methods of "detection." One of these was trial by ordeal. For example, if a woman was suspected of being a witch, she was "tried" using a ducking stool (right). If she remained conscious, people believed that spirits were protecting her, and she was burned at the stake.

## A bump on the head

An early attempt to apply science to crime was phrenology, invented by Franz Gall in 1796. Assuming (correctly) that specific areas of the brain controlled particular functions, Gall claimed that each area gave rise to distinctive bumps on the skull. A skilled phrenologist could thus "read" a person's skull and identify whether he or she was a criminal "type."

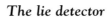

## The lie detector

Also called a polygraph, the electrical lie detector was developed in the 1930s. First, a suspect is asked various simple questions to establish a "normal" reading of the volume of air breathed, variations in blood pressure, and the amount of sweat on the skin's surface. These readings are recorded on a graph. The suspect is then asked questions about a crime and the results are compared. A marked deviation from "normal" responses may indicate that the suspect is lying.

---

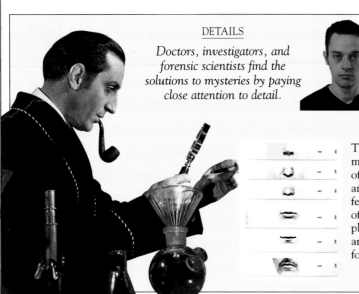

DETAILS

*Doctors, investigators, and forensic scientists find the solutions to mysteries by paying close attention to detail.*

## Photofit

Photofit kits help the police to build up a picture of a criminal's appearance.

The kit contains many examples of eyes, noses, and other facial features on pages of transparent plastic. These are combined to form a face.

The final result may be enough to jog the memories of witnesses and so lead to a conviction.

### Genetic fingerprinting
In the 1960s, it was discovered that every human cell contained a genetic code stored in the form of long strings of molecules called DNA. Only identical twins have the same DNA. Even the most minute samples of skin, hair, or blood collected from a crime scene can be analyzed to reveal a unique "genetic fingerprint" that can then be compared to that of a suspect.

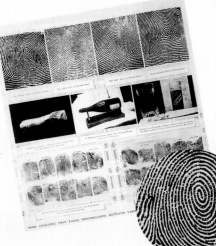

### Trace evidence
Edmond Locard was both a doctor and a lawyer. In 1910, he proposed a scientific rule of particular value to forensic science: every contact leaves a trace. Traces from a crime scene, such as microscopic drops of blood from a murder victim, will attach themselves to a criminal's skin or clothes; and traces of the criminal, such as hairs, fingerprints, or fibers from clothing will remain at the crime scene. Powerful microscopes enable forensic scientist to analyze and use these traces as evidence.

### Fingerprints
In 1858, science proved that no two persons have the same fingerprints. Dusting a crime scene for fingerprints eventually became standard police procedure. Powder is sprinkled over surfaces likely to have been touched by a criminal. The powder sticks to moisture, leaving a visible impression of a fingerprint that can be lifted off with adhesive tape. The prints are then compared to the suspect's.

### Forensic dentistry
Teeth are very durable and often survive when a corpse decomposes, enabling it to be identified. Forensic dentistry can identify the perpetrator of a crime, too. In 1906, a burglar was convicted after a piece of cheese he had bitten into at the crime scene was produced as evidence!

### Bugging
Bugs are a very effective method of surveillance. A tiny cordless microphone was once found in the model of the Great Seal above the desk of a US Ambassador. The Seal had been there for years, a gift from the Mayor of Moscow!

### CRIME PREVENTION
*Technological advances have made it fairly easy to record vital events and conversations to use as evidence to secure a conviction, while alarms of various kinds have made all sorts of crimes harder to get away with.*

### Anti-theft devices

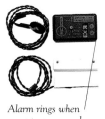

*Alarm rings when documents are moved or desk drawer is opened*

*Magnet cancels alarm*

### CCTV
Closed-circuit television means that a vulnerable site – a shopping center, a bank, a millionaire's mansion – can be kept under constant surveillance. A video camera transmits signals down a cable and sends them to a TV monitor. If a crime is committed, there will be video footage to use as evidence. While CCTV remains a deterrent to crime, some people are disturbed by the idea that someone is watching their every move.

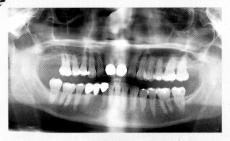

*CCTV cameras*

## Chapter one

# MR. SHERLOCK HOLMES

**Oliver Wendell Holmes**
*Sir Arthur Conan Doyle may
have named his hero after the
American essayist, physician,
and professor of anatomy,
Oliver Wendell Holmes
whom he greatly admired.*

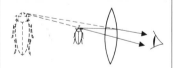

**Penang lawyer**
*This heavy stick was
so called because it was
carried for protection in
far-flung parts of the British
Empire, such as Penang in
the Malay Peninsula.*

**Convex lens**
*A convex lens curves
outward bringing light rays
together. It acts as a
magnifier producing an image
that is larger than the object
itself.*

MR. SHERLOCK HOLMES, who was usually very late in the mornings, save upon those not infrequent occasions when he stayed up all night, was seated at the breakfast table. I picked up the stick which our visitor had left behind him the night before. It was a fine, thick piece of wood, bulbous headed, known as a "Penang lawyer."

"TO JAMES MORTIMER, MRCS, FROM HIS FRIENDS OF THE CCH, 1884" was engraved on it.

"Well, Watson, what do you make of it?"

Holmes was sitting with his back to me, and I had given him no sign of my occupation.

"How did you know what I was doing? I believe you have eyes in the back of your head."

"I have, at least, a well-polished, silver-plated coffee pot in front of me," said he. "But, tell me, Watson, what do you make of our visitor's stick? Since we have been so unfortunate as to miss him and have no notion of his errand, this accidental souvenir becomes of importance. Let me hear you reconstruct the man by an examination of it."

"I think," said I, following so far as I could the methods of my companion, "that Dr. Mortimer is a successful elderly medical man, well-esteemed, since those who know him give him this mark of their appreciation."

"Good!" said Holmes. "Excellent!"

"I think he is probably a country practitioner who does a great deal of his visiting on foot."

"Why so?"

"Because this stick has been so knocked about that I can hardly imagine a town practitioner carrying it."

"Perfectly sound!" said Holmes.

"And then there is the 'friends of

the CCH.' I guess that to be the Something Hunt, the local hunt to whose members he has possibly given some surgical assistance, and which made him a small presentation in return."

"Really, Watson, you excel yourself," said Holmes, pushing back his chair and lighting a cigarette. "You habitually underrate your abilities. It may be that you are not yourself luminous, but you are a conductor of light. Some people without possessing genius have a remarkable power of stimulating it. I confess, my dear fellow, that I am very much in your debt."

He had never said as much before, and his words gave me keen pleasure.

He took the stick to the window, and looked at it with a convex lens.

"Interesting, though elementary," said he.

*"I have, at least, a well-polished, silver-plated coffee pot in front of me."*

*I took down the Medical Directory and looked up the name.*

"Has anything escaped me?" I asked, with some self-importance.

"I am afraid, my dear Watson, that most of your conclusions were erroneous. Not that you were entirely wrong. The man is certainly a country practitioner. However, a presentation to a doctor is more likely to come from a hospital than from a hunt, and when the initials "CC" are placed before that hospital the words "Charing Cross" suggest themselves."

"You may be right. But what further inferences may we draw?"

"You know my methods. Apply them!"

"I can only think that the man has practiced in town before going to the country."

"I think we might venture further. On what occasion would such a presentation be made? At the moment when Dr. Mortimer left the hospital to start his own practice. We know there has been a presentation. We believe there has been a change from a town hospital to a country practice. Is it stretching our inference too far to say that the presentation was on the occasion of the change?"

"It certainly seems probable."

"Now, he could not have been on the staff of the hospital, since only a man well established in a London practice could hold such a position, and such a one would not drift into the country. If he was in the hospital and yet not on the staff, he must have been little more than a senior student. And he left five years ago – the date is on the stick. So there emerges a young fellow under thirty, amiable, unambitious, absent-minded, and the possessor of a dog, which I owe is larger than a terrier and smaller than a mastiff."

I laughed incredulously as Sherlock Holmes leaned back in his settee and blew little wavering rings of smoke up to the ceiling.

From my medical shelf I took down the Medical Directory and looked up the name.

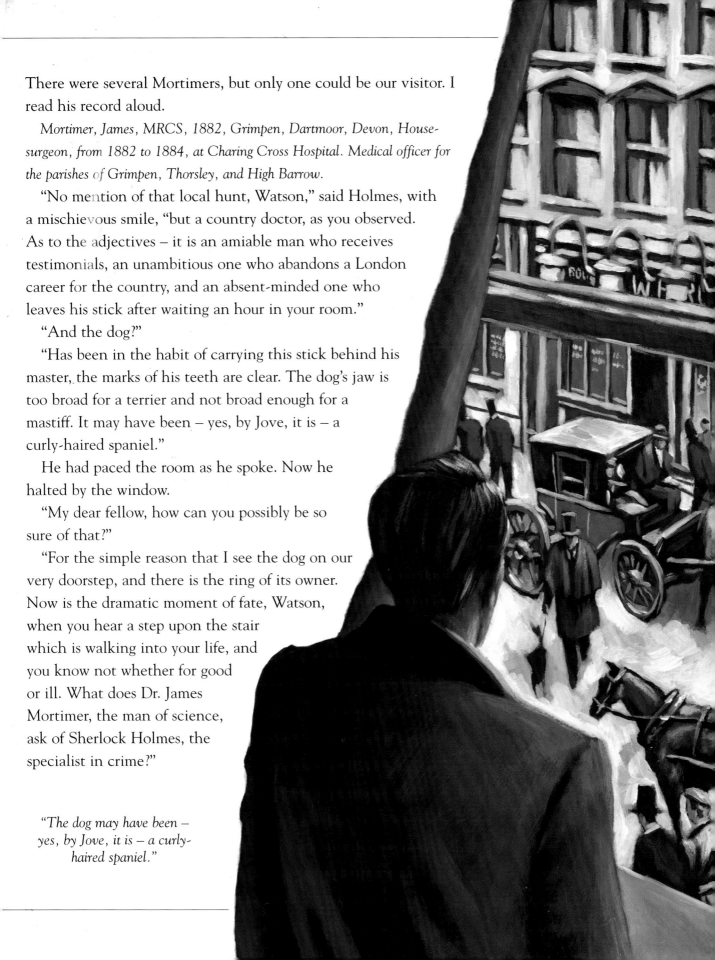

There were several Mortimers, but only one could be our visitor. I read his record aloud.

*Mortimer, James, MRCS, 1882, Grimpen, Dartmoor, Devon, House-surgeon, from 1882 to 1884, at Charing Cross Hospital. Medical officer for the parishes of Grimpen, Thorsley, and High Barrow.*

"No mention of that local hunt, Watson," said Holmes, with a mischievous smile, "but a country doctor, as you observed. As to the adjectives – it is an amiable man who receives testimonials, an unambitious one who abandons a London career for the country, and an absent-minded one who leaves his stick after waiting an hour in your room."

"And the dog?"

"Has been in the habit of carrying this stick behind his master, the marks of his teeth are clear. The dog's jaw is too broad for a terrier and not broad enough for a mastiff. It may have been – yes, by Jove, it is – a curly-haired spaniel."

He had paced the room as he spoke. Now he halted by the window.

"My dear fellow, how can you possibly be so sure of that?"

"For the simple reason that I see the dog on our very doorstep, and there is the ring of its owner. Now is the dramatic moment of fate, Watson, when you hear a step upon the stair which is walking into your life, and you know not whether for good or ill. What does Dr. James Mortimer, the man of science, ask of Sherlock Holmes, the specialist in crime?"

*"The dog may have been – yes, by Jove, it is – a curly-haired spaniel."*

Chapter two

# THE CURSE OF THE BASKERVILLES

A TALL, THIN MAN APPEARED. His eyes fell upon the stick in Holmes' hand. "I'm so glad," said he, "I would not lose that stick for the world."

"A presentation from Charing Cross Hospital?" asked Holmes.

"From one or two friends there on the occasion of my marriage."

"Dear, dear - you have disarranged our deductions."

"Yes, I married, and so left the hospital, and with it all hopes of a consulting practice."

"Come, come, we are not so far wrong after all. And now, Dr Mortimer," said Holmes, waving our visitor into a chair. "Would you kindly tell me how I can be of assistance?"

"I have in my pocket a manuscript," said Dr. Mortimer.

"I observed it as you entered the room, early eighteenth century."

"How can you say that, sir?"

"You have presented an inch or two of it to my examination. I put the date at 1730."

"The exact date is 1742." Dr. Mortimer drew it from his breastpocket. "This family paper was committed to my care by Sir Charles Baskerville, whose sudden death three months ago created much excitement in Devonshire. It is a certain legend which runs in the Baskerville family. With your permission I will read it.

" 'Long ago the Manor of Baskerville was held by Hugo, a wild and godless man. This Hugo came to love the daughter of a yeoman, but the young maiden avoided him.

'One Michaelmas, this Hugo, with his idle and wicked companions, carried off the maiden to the hall. But she escaped by the aid of the growth of ivy which covered the south wall, and set off homeward across the moor.

'Hugo declared that he would render his body and soul to the Powers of Evil to overtake the wench. He cried to his grooms to saddle his mare and unkennel his hounds, and they were off full cry into the moonlight over the moor.

'The revellers followed in pursuit. They passed a night shepherd, who was crazed with fear. He said he had seen the maiden, with the hounds upon her track.

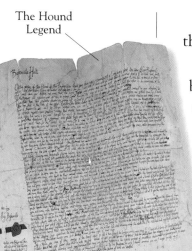

The Hound Legend

**Dating a manuscript**
*Sherlock Holmes can tell the age of a manuscript just by looking at it. The way the letters are formed, the type of paper used, and the damage it has sustained all reveal its age. Nowadays, investigators are more likely to send manuscripts to a laboratory to be chemically analyzed.*

"But I have seen more than that," he cried, "for Hugo Baskerville passed me on his black mare, and there ran mute behind him such a hound of hell as God forbid should ever be at my heels."

'A great fear came upon the revellers. They soon came upon the hounds whimpering at the head of a deep dip. The moon shone bright upon the clearing, and there lay the unhappy maid dead of fear and fatigue. But it was not the sight of her body, nor even the body of Hugo Baskerville lying near her, which raised the hair upon their heads. Standing over Hugo, picking at his throat, there stood a great, black beast, shaped like a hound, yet larger. The thing tore the throat out of Hugo Baskerville and as it turned its blazing eyes and dripping jaws upon them, they shrieked with fear and rode for dear life across the moor.

'Such is the tale of the coming of the hound, which is said to have plagued the family ever since: many have been unhappy in their deaths, which have been sudden, bloody, and mysterious. I hereby counsel you to forbear from crossing the moor in those dark hours when the powers of evil are exalted.' "

Dr. Mortimer finished reading and stared across at Mr. Sherlock Holmes.

"Do you find it interesting?"

"To a collector of fairy tales."

*A great, black beast, shaped like a hound, yet larger.*

Dr. Mortimer drew a folded newspaper out of his pocket. "This paper gives an account of the death of Sir Charles Baskerville."

*Sir Charles lay on his face, his arms out, his fingers dug into the ground, and his features convulsed into some strong emotion.*

---

**The facts of the case**
When someone dies under suspicious circumstances, a coroner is called in to investigate. Coroners have both a detailed knowledge of the law and an understanding of medical science.

'The recent death of Sir Charles Baskerville has cast a gloom over the country. The facts of the case are simple. Sir Charles Baskerville was in the habit of walking down the Yew Alley of Baskerville Hall every night. On the 4th of June, Sir Charles had declared his intention of starting the next day for London. That night he went out for his usual walk. He never returned. At 12 o'clock Barrymore, the butler, became alarmed and went in search of his master. The day had been wet and Sir Charles's footmarks were easily traced down the Alley. Halfway down this walk there is a gate which leads out onto the moor. There were indications that Sir Charles had stood for some time here. He then proceeded down the Alley, and it was at the far end of it that his body was discovered. Barrymore stated that his master's footprints altered their character from the time he passed the moor gate, and that he appeared from then onward to have been walking upon his toes. No signs of violence were discovered on Sir Charles' person, and though the doctor's evidence pointed to an *almost incredible facial distortion, it was explained that this is a symptom which is not unusual in cases of dyspnea.*

*The next-of-kin is Mr. Henry Baskerville, the son of Sir Charles Baskerville's younger brother. The young man, when last heard of, was in America.*

"Those are the public facts, Mr. Holmes."

"Then let me have the private ones."

He leaned back, put his fingertips together, and assumed his most judicial expression.

"I saw a good deal of Sir Charles Baskerville," said Dr. Mortimer.

"With the exception of Mr. Frankland of Lafter Hall, and Mr. Stapleton, the naturalist, there are no other men of education within miles. Mr. Charles had taken this legend which I have read you to heart – nothing would induce him to go out upon the moor at night. He was convinced that a dreadful fate overhung his family.

**Prints**
*A trail of footprints forms a track that can tell us the sex, age, and general condition of an animal as well as how fast it was moving. The information Holmes acquires from examining the tracks in the Yew Alley are clues he uses to solve the mystery.*

"I remember driving up to his house some three weeks before the fatal event. He was standing at the hall door, when I saw his eyes stare past me with an expression of the horror. I whisked round and caught a glimpse of something which I took to be a large black calf.

"It was at my advice that Sir Charles was about to go to London. His heart was affected, and the constant anxiety in which he lived was having a serious effect on his health.

"On the night of Sir Charles' death, Barrymore sent for me. I reached Baskerville Hall within an hour of the event. I followed the footsteps down the Yew Alley, I saw the spot at the moor gate where he seemed to have waited. I remarked the change in the shape of the prints after that point, I noted that there were no other footsteps save those of Barrymore. Sir Charles lay on his face, his arms out, his fingers dug into the ground, and his features convulsed with some strong emotion. But one false statement was made by Barrymore. He said there were no traces upon the ground around the body. He did not observe any. But I did – some distance off, but fresh and clear."

"Footprints?"

"Footprints."

"A man's or a woman's?"

Dr. Mortimer's voice sank almost to a whisper as he answered:

"Mr. Holmes, they were the footprints of a gigantic hound!"

Holmes leaned forward in his excitement.

"You saw this, and you said nothing?"

"What was the use?"

"How was it that no one else saw it?"

"The marks were some twenty yards from the body, and no one gave them a thought."

"There are many sheep dogs on the moor?"

"No doubt, but this was no sheep dog."

"What is the alley like?"

"There are two lines of old yew hedge, twelve feet high and impenetrable. The walk in the center is about eight feet across, with a strip of grass on either side."

"I understand that the yew hedge is penetrated at one point by a gate?"

"Yes, the wicket gate which leads on to the moor; there is no other opening."

"So that to reach the Yew Valley one either has to come down it from the house or else to enter it by the moor gate?"

*There are two lines of old yew hedge, twelve feet high and impenetrable.*

"There is an exit through a summer house at the far end. Sir Charles lay about fifty yards from here."

"The marks which you saw were on the path and not on the grass?"

"No marks could show on the grass."

"Were they on the same side of the path as the moor gate?"

"Yes."

"Was the wicket gate closed?"

"Closed and padlocked."

"How high was it?"

"About four feet high."

"Then anyone could have got over it. What marks did you see by the wicket gate?"

"It was all very confused. Sir Charles had evidently stood there for five or ten minutes."

"How do you know that?"

"Because the ash had dropped twice from his cigar."

"Excellent! This is a colleague, Watson, after our own heart. But the marks?"

"He had left his own marks all over that small patch of gravel. I could discern no others."

**The Yew Alley**
*Pictured above are the Yew Alley and Summer House Sir Arthur Conan Doyle may have been thinking of when he wrote this story. They are at Stoneyhurst College, where he went to school.*

Sherlock Holmes struck his hand against his knee with an impatient gesture. "If only I had been there! Oh, Dr. Mortimer, why did you hesitate to call me in?"

"There is a realm in which the most acute and experienced of detectives is helpless."

"You mean that the thing is supernatural?"

"Before the terrible event occurred, several people had seen a creature upon the moor – exactly corresponding to the hell-hound of the legend."

"And you believe it to be supernatural?"

"I do not know what to believe."

Holmes shrugged his shoulders. "I have hitherto confined my investigations to this world. In a modest way I have combated evil, but to take on the Father of Evil himself would, perhaps, be too ambitious a task. Yet you must admit that the footmark is material."

"The original hound was material enough to tug a man's throat out, and yet he was diabolical as well."

"I see that you have quite gone over to the supernaturalists. But now, Dr. Mortimer, tell me this. If you hold these views, why have you come to consult me at all?"

"To advise me as to what I should do with Sir Henry Baskerville, who arrives at Waterloo Station," Dr. Mortimer looked at his watch, "in exactly one hour and a quarter."

**Yellow fever**
*This disease occurs in hot countries and is transmitted by the bite of female mosquitoes belonging to the species* Aedes aegypti. *A vaccine is effective, but there is no known cure.*

Tobacco jar

Cigarettes

Tobacco leaf

MARTENIEK

Cigars    Pipes    Cigar cutter

**Tobacco**
*Smoking was popular among Victorian men of all classes, and all kinds of smoking-related products were made. Nicotine, a chemical contained in tobacco, is poisonous, but also a stimulant. Holmes smokes to help him think when faced with a difficult case.*

"He being the heir?"

"Yes. On the death of Sir Charles we inquired for this young gentleman, and found that he had been farming in Canada."

"There is no other claimant, I presume?"

"None. Rodger Baskerville, the youngest of three brothers, of whom Sir Charles was the eldest, died of yellow fever in Central America. The second brother, who died young, is the father of Henry, the last of the Baskervilles. Mr. Holmes, what should I do?"

"I recommend, sir, that you proceed to Waterloo to meet Sir Henry Baskerville. At ten o'clock tomorrow, call upon me here, and bring him with you. One more question. You say that before Sir Charles Baskervilles' death several people saw this apparition upon the moor?"

"Three people did," Dr. Mortimer replied.

"Did any see it after?"

"I have not heard of any."

"Thank you. Good morning."

I knew that seclusion and solitude were very necessary for my friend in those hours of intense concentration during which he weighed every particle of evidence. I therefore spent the day at my club, and did not return to Baker Street until evening.

As I opened the door, acrid tobacco fumes took me by the throat and set me coughing. Holmes was in his dressing gown coiled up in an armchair with his black clay pipe between his lips.

"Caught cold, Watson?" said he.

"No, it's this poisonous atmosphere."

"Open the window, then! I have been to Devonshire, Watson."

"In spirit?"

"Exactly. My body has remained in this armchair, and has consumed two large pots of coffee and an incredible amount of tobacco. I sent down to Stanford's for the map of this portion of the moor, and my spirit has hovered over it all day." He unrolled one section. "This is the stage upon which tragedy has been played."

"It must be a wild place."

"Yes, the setting is a worthy one. What do you make of the case?

That change in the footprints, for example?"

"Mortimer said that the man had walked on tiptoe."

"He only repeated what some fool had said at the inquest. Why should a man walk on tiptoe down the alley? He was running, Watson – running for his life."

"Running from what?"

"There lies our problem. Presuming that the cause of his fear came across the moor, only a man who had lost his wits would have run from the house instead of toward it. Then again, why was he waiting in the Yew Alley?"

"You think he was waiting for someone?"

"The man was elderly and the night was inclement. Is it natural that he should stand for five or ten minutes? It was the night before he was to depart for London. Hand me my violin, and we will postpone further thought until we have met with Dr. Mortimer and Sir Henry Baskerville in the morning."

*As I opened the door, acrid tobacco fumes took me by the throat.*

**Late Victorian style**
*This traveling clock is typical of the late-Victorian fashion for elaborate decoration – which helps make the world of the Sherlock Holmes stories so attractive to modern eyes.*

SIR HENRY BASKERVILLE,
NORTHUMBERLAND HOTEL

Chapter three

# SIR HENRY BASKERVILLE

THE CLOCK HAD JUST STRUCK TEN when Dr. Mortimer was shown up followed by the young baronet, an alert dark-eyed man, sturdily built.

"I understand, Mr. Sherlock Holmes," said he, "that you think out little puzzles, and I've had one this morning."

He laid an envelope upon the table. The address, SIR HENRY BASKERVILLE, NORTHUMBERLAND HOTEL, was printed in rough characters; the postmark "Charing Cross," and the date of posting the preceding evening.

"Who knew that you were going to the Northumberland Hotel?" asked Holmes.

"No one. We only decided after I met Dr. Mortimer."

"But Dr. Mortimer was, no doubt, already stopping there?"

"No, I had been staying with a friend," said the doctor.

"Hum! Someone seems to be very deeply interested in your movements." Out of the envelope he took a paper. Across the middle of it a single sentence had been formed by pasting printed words upon it:

as you value your life or your reason keep away from the *moor*

"Might I trouble you for yesterday's *Times*, Watson?" Holmes glanced swiftly over it, running his eyes up and down the columns. "Capital article, this, on Free Trade."

'You may be cajoled into imagining that your own special trade or your own industry will be encouraged by a protective tariff, but it stands to reason that such legistlation must in the long run keep away wealth from the country, diminish the value of our imports, and lower the general conditions of life in this island.'

"What do you think of that, Watson?" cried Holmes.

Sir Henry Baskerville turned a pair of puzzled dark eyes upon me. "I don't know much about the tariff, but it seems to me we've got a bit off the trail so far as that note is concerned."

"On the contrary, I think we are hot upon the trail, Sir Henry. Watson here knows more about my methods than you do, but I fear that even he has not quite grasped the significance of this sentence."

"No, I confess that I see no connection."

"And yet, my dear Watson, there is so very close a connection that the one is extracted out of the other. "YOU," "YOUR," "LIFE," "REASON," "VALUE," "KEEP AWAY," "FROM THE." Don't you see now whence these words have been taken?"

"Really, Mr. Holmes, this exceeds anything which I could have imagined,"said Dr Mortimer. "How did you do it?"

"The detection of types is one of the most elementary branches of knowledge to the special expert in crime. A *Times* leader is entirely distinctive, and these words could have been taken from nothing else. As it was done yesterday the strong probability was that we should find the words in yesterday's issue."

"But I want to know," said Sir Henry Baskerville, "why the word 'moor' should have been written?"

"Because he could not find it in print."

"That would explain it. Have you read anything else in this message, Mr. Holmes?"

"The address is printed in rough characters. But *The Times* is a paper which is seldom found in any hands but those of the highly educated. Therefore, the letter was composed by an educated man who wished to pose as an uneducated one, and his effort to conceal his own writing suggests that that writing might be known, or come to be known, by you. Now, I am almost certain that this address has been written in an hotel. Both the pen and the ink have given the writer trouble. The pen has spluttered twice in a single word, and has run dry three times, showing that there was very little ink in the bottle. A private pen or ink bottle is seldom allowed to be in such a state, and the combination of the two must be quite rare. But you know the hotel ink and the hotel pen, where it is rare to get anything else. Hullo, what's this?" He was carefully examining the foolscap, holding it only an inch or two from his eyes.

"Well?"

"Nothing," said he, throwing it down. "It is a blank sheet of paper, without even a watermark on it. And now, Sir Henry, has anything else of interest happened to you since you have been in London?"

***Dressing gown***
*A dressing gown was an important part of Holmes' image. It marked him out as a man of independent means (he could afford to lounge about his flat all day) and also as slightly eccentric.*

Sir Henry smiled. "I hope that to lose one of your brand new boots is not part of the routine over here. I put them outside my door last night, and there was only one in the morning."

"If you have never worn them, why did you put them out to be cleaned?"

"They were tan boots and had not yet been varnished. I did a good deal of shopping. You see, if I am to be squire I must dress the part."

"It seems a singularly useless thing to steal," said Sherlock Holmes. "We now have to decide, Sir Henry, whether or not it is advisable for you to go to Baskerville Hall."

"My answer is fixed. No man on earth can prevent me from going to the home of my own people." His brows knitted and his face flushed. It was evident that the fiery temper of the Baskervilles was not extinct in this, their last representative. "Meanwhile, I will go back to my hotel. Suppose you and Dr. Watson come round and lunch with us at two?"

"We will meet again. Good morning!"

We heard our visitors leave and bang the front door. Holmes changed from the languid dreamer to the man of action.

"Your hat and boots, Watson, quick!" He rushed into his room in his dressing gown and was back in a few seconds in a frock coat. We hurried down the stairs and into the street.

Dr. Mortimer and Baskerville were still visible ahead of us.

"Shall I run on and stop them?"

"Not for the world, my dear Watson."

He quickened his pace. Our friends stopped at a shop window. A hansom cab halted on the other side of the street, then continued.

"There's our man, Watson! Come along!"

I was aware of a bushy black beard and a pair of piercing eyes turned upon us through the side window of the cab. Instantly the trap-door at the top flew up, something was screamed to the driver, and the cab flew madly off. Holmes dashed in wild pursuit amid the stream of traffic, but already the cab was out of sight.

"Who was the man – a spy?"

"Well, it was evident that Baskerville has been very closely shadowed by someone since he has been in town."

"What a pity we did not get the number of the cab!"

"My dear Watson, 2704 is our man. Could you swear to his face?"

"I could swear only to the beard."

"And so could I – from which I gather that in all probability it was a false one."

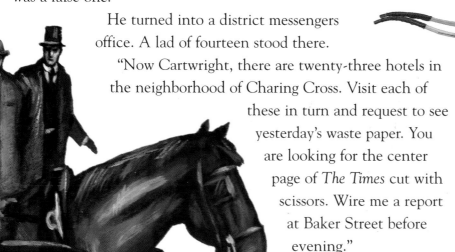

He turned into a district messengers office. A lad of fourteen stood there.

"Now Cartwright, there are twenty-three hotels in the neighborhood of Charing Cross. Visit each of these in turn and request to see yesterday's waste paper. You are looking for the center page of *The Times* cut with scissors. Wire me a report at Baker Street before evening."

**Squire**
The title "Squire" is passed from father to son. The squire is the principal landowner in a country district. Before the 19th century he also used to govern the local people.

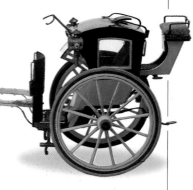

**Getting around town**
At the end of the 19th century, cars had barely been invented, and horse-drawn hansom cabs (above) were the taxis of the time. In 1903, Sir Arthur Conan Doyle became one of the first private motorists on the roads in Britain.

*I was aware of a bushy black beard and a pair of piercing eyes turned upon us.*

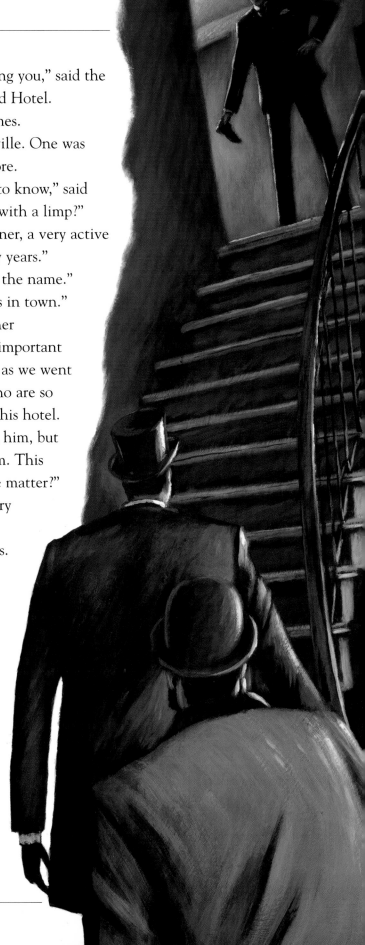

"Sir Henry Baskerville is upstairs expecting you," said the clerk when we reached the Northumberland Hotel.

"May I look at your register?" asked Holmes.

Two names had been added after Baskerville. One was Theophilus Johnson, the other Mrs. Oldmore.

"Surely that must be the Johnson I used to know," said Holmes, "a lawyer, gray-headed, and walks with a limp?"

"No, sir, this is Mr. Johnson, the coal-owner, a very active gentleman. He has used this hotel for many years."

"Mrs. Oldmore, too. I seem to remember the name."

"An invalid who comes to us when she is in town."

"Thank you; I am afraid I cannot claim her acquaintance. We have established a most important fact, Watson," he continued in a low voice as we went upstairs. "We know now that the people who are so interested in our friend have not settled in his hotel. That means that they are anxious to watch him, but equally anxious that he should not see them. This suggests – hello, my dear fellow, what is the matter?"

We had run up against a flushed Sir Henry Baskerville clutching an old, dusty boot.

"Still looking for your boot?" said Holmes.

"Yes, sir, and mean to find it."

"But you said it was a new brown boot?"

"So it was, sir. And now it's an old black one. Last night they took one of my brown ones, and today they have sneaked one of the black. It's the maddest, queerest thing that ever happened to me."

"The queerest, perhaps," mused Holmes.

After lunch Sir Henry announced his intention to go to Baskerville Hall at the end of the week.

"I think your decision is wise," said Holmes.

*A flushed Sir Henry Baskerville clutched an old, dusty boot.*

"Did you know, Dr Mortimer, that you were followed today?"

Dr Mortimer started. "By whom?"

"That, I cannot tell you. Have you among your Dartmoor acquaintances a man with a black, full beard?"

"No – or, let me see – why, yes. Barrymore, Sir Charles' butler who is in charge of the Hall has a full, black beard."

"We must send a telegraph to be delivered into his own hand and await the reply. We should know before evening whether Barrymore is in Devonshire or not. Did Barrymore profit by Sir Charles' will?"

"He and his wife had five hundred pounds each. I hope," Dr. Mortimer continued, "that you do not look with suspicious eyes upon everyone who received a legacy from Sir Charles, for I also had a thousand pounds left to me."

"Indeed!" said Holmes. "And anyone else?"

"The residue, seven hundred and forty thousand pounds, went to Sir Henry."

Holmes raised his eyebrows. "A sum for which a man might play a desperate game. One more question, Dr. Mortimer: suppose anything happened to our young friend here – who would inherit the estate?"

"The estate would descend to a distant cousin, James Desmond, an elderly clergyman."

"And have you made your will, Sir Henry?"

"Not yet – only yesterday did I learn how matters stood."

"Well, Sir Henry, I agree with your going to Devonshire without delay, but you must take a companion with you." Holmes laid his hand upon my arm. "I will come with pleasure," said I.

We had risen to depart when Baskerville gave a cry of triumph and drew a brown boot from under a cabinet.

"My missing boot!" he cried.

"May all our difficulties vanish as easily!" said Holmes.

A boy working as a shoeblack in the Liverpool docks in 1895.

**Telegraph**
*This telegraph machine allowed messages to be translated into radio or electrical signals and transmitted along a wire. At the other end, the signals were translated back into words and the message delivered.*

Holmes sat in silence in the cab as we drove back to Baker Street. All afternoon and late into the evening he sat lost in tobacco and thought. Just before dinner two telegrams were handed in:

> HAVE JUST HEARD THAT BARRYMORE IS AT THE HALL – BASKERVILLE

> VISITED 23 HOTELS AS DIRECTED, BUT SORRY TO REPORT UNABLE TO TRACE CUT SHEET OF TIMES – CARTWRIGHT

"Nothing is more stimulating than a case where everything goes against you, Watson."

"We still have the cabman who drove the spy."

"Exactly. I have wired the Official Registry for his name and address. I should not be surprised if this were my answer." The ring at the bell proved to be something even more satisfactory, for the door opened and a rough-looking fellow entered. "I got a message from the head office," said he. "I've driven my cab for seven years and never a word

*Never have I seen my friend more completely taken aback than by the cabman's reply.*

of complaint. I came straight here to ask what you had against me."

"I have nothing in the world against you, my good man. On the contrary, I have half a sovereign for you if you will answer my questions. Now, tell me about the fare who watched this house this morning and then followed two gentlemen down Regent Street."

The man looked surprised and a little embarrassed. "The gentleman told me he was a detective, and that I was to say nothing about him to anyone."

"My good fellow, you may find yourself in a pretty bad position if you try to hide anything from me. Did he say anything more?"

"He mentioned his name."

Holmes cast a swift glance of triumph at me.

"Oh, he mentioned his name, did he? What was the name that he mentioned?"

"His name," said the cabman, "was Mr. Sherlock Holmes."

Never have I seen my friend more completely taken aback than by the cabman's reply. For an instant he sat in silent amazement. Then he burst into a hearty laugh.

"A touch, Watson – an undeniable touch!" said he. "So his name was Sherlock Holmes, was it? Excellent! Tell me all that occurred."

"He hailed me in Trafalgar Square and offered me two guineas if I would do what he wanted and ask no questions. First we drove down to the Northumberland Hotel and waited there until two gentlemen came out and took a cab. We followed their cab until it pulled up here. We waited until the two gentlemen passed us, and we followed down Baker Street and along –"

"I know," said Holmes.

"Until we got three-quarters down Regent Street. Then he cried that I should drive to Waterloo Station. We were there in ten minutes, and away he went."

"And how would you describe Mr. Sherlock Holmes?"

The cabman scratched his head. "I'd say he was forty, and of a middle height. He was dressed like a toff, with a black beard and a pale face. I don't know as I could say more than that."

"Well, then, here is your half-sovereign. There's another one waiting if you can bring any more information. Good night!"

"Good night, sir, and thank you!"

Holmes turned to me with a rueful smile. "The cunning rascal! I've been checkmated in London. I can only wish you better luck in Devonshire. But I'm not easy in my mind about sending you. It's an ugly, dangerous business. Yes, I give you my word that I shall be very glad to have you back safe and sound in Baker Street once more."

Shilling

Half sovereign

Sovereign: worth one pound

**Victorian money**
A "guinea" meant one pound and one shilling. No guinea coins had been made after 1813, but the term was still in common use.

Chapter Four

# Baskerville Hall

SIR HENRY BASKERVILLE and Dr. Mortimer were ready upon the appointed day, and we started for Devonshire. Mr. Sherlock Holmes gave me his last parting advice.

"I will not bias your mind by suggesting theories or suspicions, Watson," said he. "Simply report the facts in the fullest possible manner, and leave me to do the theorizing."

"I will do my best."

"Well, goodbye," he said, as the train began to glide down the station platform. "Bear in mind, Sir Henry, one of the phrases in that old legend, and avoid the moor in those hours of darkness when the powers of evil are exalted."

**Princetown**
*This prison was set up in western Dartmoor in 1802 to house French prisoners during the Napoleonic war. It later become Britain's best-known prison for long-term convicts.*

I looked back at the platform when we had left it far behind, and saw the tall figure of Holmes standing motionless and gazing after us.

The journey was a swift and pleasant one. Young Baskerville stared eagerly out at the Devon scenery.

"There is your first sight of the moor," said Dr. Mortimer, pointing out of the carriage window. There rose in the distance a gray, melancholy hill, with a strange jagged summit, dim and vague in the distance, like some fantastic landscape in a dream. Baskerville sat for a long time, his eyes fixed upon it.

The train pulled up. Outside, a wagonette was waiting, and in a few minutes we were flying swiftly down the white road.

*Two high, narrow towers rose up.*
*"Baskerville Hall" said the coachman.*

Behind the peaceful sunlit countryside there rose dark against the evening sky the long gloomy curve of the moor.

"Hullo!" cried Dr. Mortimer, "What is this?"

Steep heath-clad land lay in front of us. On the summit was a mounted soldier, his rifle poised ready over his forearm.

"There is a convict escaped from Princetown, sir," said our driver. "It is Selden, the Notting Hill murderer."

I remembered the case well, on account of the ferocity of the crime. Somewhere on the desolate plain was lurking this fiendish man, hiding in a burrow like a wild beast.

The road in front of us grew bleaker and wilder. Suddenly we looked down into a cup-like depression, patched with stunted oaks and firs which had been twisted and bent by the fury of years of storm. Two high, narrrow towers rose up.

"Baskerville Hall," said the coachman.

Its master had risen, and was staring with flushed cheeks and shining eyes.

Black Tor, Dartmoor

**Granite tors**
*Dartmoor's summits are called tors – formations of granite that remained after softer rocks had been worn away by wind and weather.*

### On the staff

*A large house such as Baskerville Hall required many servants. Baskerville Hall, however, is modestly staffed, with just a butler, a housekeeper, a maid or two, and a kitchen boy.*

A Victorian housemaid

A few minutes later we had reached the lodge gates. Baskerville shuddered as he looked up the long, dark drive to where the house glimmered like a ghost at the farther end.

"Was it here?" he asked, in a low voice.

"No, the Yew Alley is on the other side."

The avenue opened into a broad expanse of turf, and the house lay before us. In the fading light I could see a heavy block of building from which a porch projected. The whole front was draped in ivy. From the central block rose the twin towers.

"Welcome, Sir Henry! Welcome to Baskerville Hall!"

A tall man had stepped from the shadow of the porch to open the door of the wagonette. The figure of a woman was silhouetted against the yellow light of the hall.

"You don't mind my driving straight home, Sir Henry?" said Dr. Mortimer.

"Barrymore will be a better guide to the house than I. Goodbye, and never hesitate to send for me if I can be of service."

The wheels died away down the drive while Sir Henry and I turned into the hall. It was a fine apartment - large, lofty, and heavily raftered with age-blackened oak.

Barrymore returned from taking our luggage to our rooms. "My wife and I will be happy, Sir Henry, to stay with you until you have made fresh arrangements."

"Do you mean that your wife and you wish to leave?"

"Only when it is convenient to you, sir."

"But your family have been with us for several generations, have they not? I should be sorry to begin my life here by breaking an old family connection."

"I feel that also, sir, and so does my wife. But we were both very much attached to Sir Charles, and his death gave us a shock and made these surroundings very painful to us."

"But what do you intend to do?"

"I have no doubt, sir, that we shall succeed in establishing ourselves in some business. Sir Charles' generosity has given us the means to do so. And now, sir, perhaps I had best show you to your rooms."

That night I found myself weary and yet wakeful, seeking sleep which would not come. Suddenly there came a sound to my ears, clear and unmistakable. It was the sob of a woman, torn by an uncontrollable sorrow. I sat up in bed and listened intently, but there came no other sound save the chiming clock and the rustle of the ivy on the wall.

*In the fading light I could see a heavy block of building from which a porch projected.*

**Butterfly hunting**
*Many Victorians were
amateur naturalists, studying
and classifying local animals
and plants. People who
collect butterflies are called
lepidopterists.*

At breakfast the following morning, I asked Sir Henry if he had heard a woman sobbing in the night.

"When I was half asleep, I fancy I heard something of the sort," said he. He asked Barrymore whether he could account for it.

"There are only two women in the house, Sir Henry," he answered, "One is the scullery-maid, who sleeps in the other wing. The other is my wife, and the sound did not come from her."

And yet he lied, for it chanced that after breakfast I met Mrs. Barrymore, and her eyes were red. It was she, then, who wept in the night, and her husband must know it. Was it possible that it was Barrymore whom we had seen in the cab in Regent Street? I decided to visit the Grimpen postmaster, and find whether our telegram had been placed in Barrymore's own hands.

It was a pleasant walk along the edge of the moor to the postmaster's house. "Did you see Barrymore when you delivered the telegram?" I asked the postmaster.

"No, sir. I gave it to Mrs. Barrymore."

Suddenly I heard running feet and I saw a small slim man. A tin box for botanical specimens hung over his shoulder, and he carried a green butterfly-net.

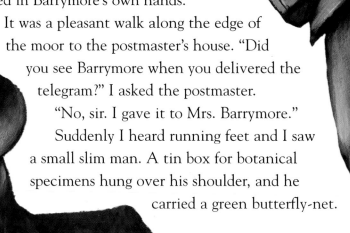

*I heard running feet,
and I saw a small,
slim man.*

"Excuse me, Dr. Watson," said he, "you may have heard of me from our friend, Mortimer. I am Stapleton of Merripit House. I was calling on Mortimer and he pointed you out. I trust Sir Henry is none the worse for his journey? We feared that after the sad death of Sir Charles he might refuse to live here. You know the legend of the fiend dog which haunts the family?"

"I have heard of it."

"The story took a great hold upon the imagination of Sir Charles, and I have no doubt that it led to his tragic end. I fancy that he really did see something that last night. I feared that some disaster might occur, for I knew, from Mortimer, that his heart was weak."

"You think then, that some dog pursued Sir Charles, and that he died of fright?"

"Has Mr Sherlock Holmes any better explanation?"

The words took away my breath.

"It is useless for us to pretend that we do not know you, Dr. Watson," said he. "If you are here, it follows that Mr. Sherlock Holmes is interesting himself in the matter. A moderate walk brings us to Merripit House, will you come and meet my sister?"

We turned together down the moor path.

"It is a wonderful place, the moor," said he, gazing over the undulating downs. "You cannot think the wonderful secrets which it contains. It is so vast, so barren, and so mysterious."

"You know it well, then?"

"I have only been here two years. But my tastes led me to explore every part – there are one or two paths, which a very active man can take. It is where the rare plants and butterflies are. You see this great plain to the north here, that is the great Grimpen Mire. A false step yonder means certain death. Only yesterday I saw a moor pony wander into it. By George, there is another of those miserable ponies!"

Something brown was tossing among the green sedges. An agonized writhing and the creature was gone. A long, low moan, indescribably sad, swept over the moor. I looked round, with a chill of fear in my heart.

"The peasants say it is the Hound of the Baskervilles calling for its prey," said Stapleton.

**Dartmoor pony**
*There are still wild or semi-wild ponies on Dartmoor, but they have undergone a great deal of change, having interbred with other horses. The main characteristic of the Dartmoor pony was its resistance to wet and cold.*

**The poor folk**
*In medieval times, most country people worked for the local landowner and, in return, received a home and some land of their own to cultivate. Even in the 19th century, "the poor folk" looked to the local squire for employment.*

A moth fluttered across our path, and in an instant Stapleton was in pursuit. The creature flew straight for the great Mire, but my acquaintance never paused for an instant, bounding behind it, his green net waving in the air.

Then I heard the sound of steps, and found a woman near me upon the path. "Go back!" she said. "Go straight back to London, instantly."

I could only stare at her in surprise. "Why should I go back?"

"I cannot explain, but for God's sake do what I ask you. Hush, my brother is coming! Not a word of what I have said."

"Hullo, Beryl!" said he, and it seemed to me that his tone was not a cordial one. "You have introduced yourselves, I see."

"Yes, I was telling Sir Henry that it was rather late for him to see the true beauties of the moor."

"No, no," said I. "My name is Dr. Watson."

A flush of vexation passed over her expressive face. "We have been talking at cross purposes, But you will come on, will you not, and see Merripit House?"

A short walk brought us to a bleak, moorland house. I wondered what could have brought this highly educated man and this beautiful woman to live in such a place.

"Queer spot to choose, is it not?" said he. "And yet we manage to make ourselves happy, do we not, Beryl?"

"Quite happy," said she, but there was no ring of conviction in her words.

"I had a school in the north country," said Stapleton. "An epidemic broke out, and three of the boys died. The school never recovered from the blow, and much of my capital was swallowed up. But I find an unlimited field of work here, and my sister is as devoted to Nature as I am. We have our books, our studies, and we have interesting neighbors. Dr. Mortimer is a most learned man. Poor Sir Charles was also an admirable companion. We knew him well, and miss him more than I can tell. Do you think that I should intrude if I were to call and make the acquaintance of Sir Henry?"

"I am sure that he would be delighted."

I resisted all pressure to stay for lunch, as I was eager to get back to my charge. I set off at once, taking the grass-grown path by which we had come. However, before I had reached the road I was astounded to see Miss Stapleton sitting upon a rock by the side of the track.

"I wanted to say to you how sorry I am about the stupid mistake I made in thinking that you were Sir Henry," said she. "Please forget the words I said."

"But I can't forget them, Miss Stapleton," said I. "I am Sir Henry's friend, and his welfare is a very close concern of mine. Tell me why it was that you were so eager that Sir Henry should return to London."

Her eyes hardened when she answered me. "You make too much of it, Dr. Watson. My brother and I were shocked by the death of Sir Charles. We knew him intimately, for his favorite walk was over the moor to our house. He was deeply impressed with the curse which hung over his family, and when this tragedy came I felt that there must be some grounds for the fears he had expressed. I was distressed, therefore, when another member of the family came to live here, and I felt that he should be warned of the danger."

"But what is the danger?"

"You know the story of the hound?"

"I do not believe in such nonsense."

"But I do. If you have any influence with Sir Henry, take him away from this place."

"If you meant no more than this, why should you not wish your brother to overhear?"

"My brother is very anxious to have the Hall inhabited, for he thinks that it is good for the poor folk upon the moor. He would be very angry if he knew that I had said anything which might induce Sir Henry to go away. But I must get back, or he will miss me and suspect that I have seen you. Goodbye!"

She turned and disappeared among the scattered boulders, while I, with my soul full of vague fears, pursued my way to Baskerville Hall.

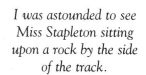

*I was astounded to see Miss Stapleton sitting upon a rock by the side of the track.*

## Chapter Five

# Dr. WATSON REPORTS

Baskerville Hall, October 13th

My Dear Holmes,

My previous letters have kept you up-to-date as to all that has occurred. There is strong reason to believe that the escaped convict that I mentioned has got right away. I have had uneasy moments when I have thought of the Stapletons, who live miles from any help. They would be helpless in the hands of a desperate fellow like this Notting Hill criminal.

"Stapleton came over to call upon Baskerville and took us both to the spot where the legend of the wicked Hugo is supposed to have had its origin. We found a short valley between rugged tors, which led to an open, grassy space. In the middle of it rose two great stones, worn and sharpened at the upper end, until they looked like the fangs of some monstrous beast. Sir Henry asked Stapleton whether he believed in the supernatural. Stapleton was guarded in his replies, but he told us of similar cases where families had suffered from some evil influence, and he left us with the impression that he shared the popular view.

On our way back we stayed for lunch at Merripit House, and Sir Henry made the acquaintance of Miss Stapleton. He appeared to be strongly attracted by her, and I am much mistaken if the feeling was not mutual. Since then hardly a day has passed that we have not seen the brother

**Country criminals**
*Conan Doyle set his story in the countryside – for centuries a place where criminals hid from the law. On country roads lurked highwaymen such as Dick Turpin (below), who held up carriages and robbed travelers at gunpoint.*

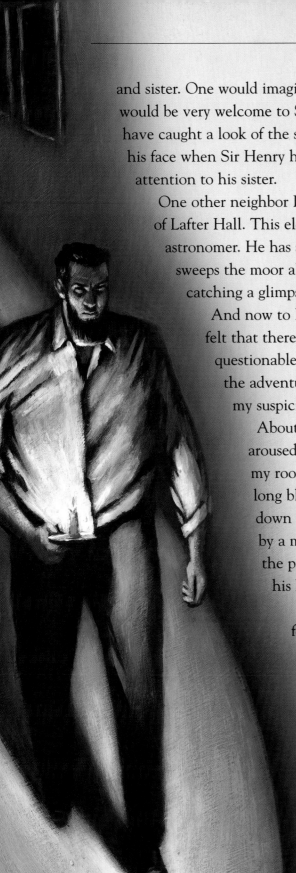

and sister. One would imagine that such a match would be very welcome to Stapleton, and yet I have caught a look of the strongest disapproval in his face when Sir Henry has been paying some attention to his sister.

One other neighbor I have met is Mr. Frankland of Lafter Hall. This elderly man is an amateur astronomer. He has an excellent telescope, and sweeps the moor all day in the hope of catching a glimpse of the escaped convict.

And now to Barrymore. I have always felt that there was something questionable in this man's character, but the adventure of last night brings all my suspicions to a head.

About two in the morning, I was aroused by a stealthy step passing my room. I rose and peeped out. A long black shadow was trailing down the corridor. It was thrown by a man who walked softly down the passage with a candle held in his hand. It was Barrymore.

I waited until he had passed out of sight, and then I followed him. I could see from the glimmer of light through an open door that he had entered one of the rooms. I crept down the passage and peeped round the corner of the door.

Barrymore was crouching at the window with the candle held against the glass, staring out into the blackness of the moor. Then he gave a groan and put out the light. I made my way back to the room, and very shortly came his stealthy steps on their return journey. What it all means I cannot guess, but there is some secret business in this house of gloom.

### New horizons
Technology was making huge advances in optical instruments at this time and people were fascinated by the possibilities the latest telescopes opened up for gazing at the stars, or simply looking at the view.

*A long black shadow was trailing down the corridor.*

**Love interest**
*It is rare in a Sherlock Holmes story that there is a female "love interest." However, Beryl Stapleton's romantic aura is a key element of the plot.*

**Emotional battleground**
*In books, plays, films, and art highly emotional scenes are often set in wild places, such as moors or heaths.*

Baskerville Hall, October 15th

My Dear Holmes

I have seldom seen a man more infatuated with a woman than Sir Henry is with Miss Stapleton. This morning, he put on his hat and prepared to go out. As a matter of course I did the same.

"Are you coming, Watson?" he asked, looking at me curiously.

"Well, you heard how earnestly Holmes insisted I should not leave you, and that you should not go alone upon the moor."

Sir Henry put his hand upon my shoulder, with a pleasant smile. "My dear fellow," said he, "Holmes, did not foresee everything. You would not wish to be a spoil-sport. Let me go out alone."

I was at a loss what to say or do. Before I had made up my mind he picked up his cane and was gone. But my conscience reproached me, so I set off at once in the direction of Merripit House.

Hurrying along, I mounted a hill from which I could see the moor. Sir Henry was walking, deep in conversation with a lady by his side who could only be Miss Stapleton. The couple had halted on the path, when I was suddenly aware that I was not their only witness. A man was moving in their direction among the broken ground. It was Stapleton with his butterfly net. At this instant, Sir Henry drew Miss Stapleton to his side. His arm was round her, but she was straining away from him. Next, they sprang apart and turned around. Stapleton was running wildly toward them. He gesticulated excitedly, then beckoned to his sister, who, after a glance at Sir Henry, joined him. The baronet walked back the way he had come. I ran down the hill and met him, his face flushed with anger.

"Watson! Where have you dropped from?"

I explained everything.

"I always thought that brother of hers sane, until today. What would prevent me from making her a good husband? He would not even let me touch the tips of her fingers."

"Did he say so?"

"That, and more. He has never let us get together, and today for the first time I saw a chance of speaking to her alone. She was glad to meet me, but would not talk of love. She insisted that this was a place of danger, and she would never be happy until I had left. I told her that I was in no hurry to leave and offered to marry her, but before she could answer down came her brother, white with rage. What was I doing? How dared I offer her attentions? I told him that I hoped that she might honor me by becoming my wife."

That afternoon, Stapleton apologized. "His sister is everything to him," Sir Henry told me later. "He recognized how foolish it was to imagine that he could always hold her to himself. He agreed to withdraw all opposition if I would let the matter rest for three months, and simply cultivate the lady's friendship. This I promised."

*His arm was round her, but she was straining away from him.*

**Hue and cry**
*These words come from the Old French meaning "to shout." They refer to a proclamation asking people to hunt down an escaped prisoner.*

Now I pass on to the sobs in the night, Mrs. Barrymore's tear-stained face, and the secret journey of the butler to the window.

Before breakfast I examined the room Barrymore had occupied. Its window had the best outlook onto the moor in the house. He had been looking out for something or somebody upon the moor.

I told the baronet what I had seen. He was less surprised than I had expected.

"I knew that Barrymore walked about at night" said he. "We should shadow him, and see what he is after."

"But surely he would hear us."

"The man is rather deaf, and in any case we must take our chance of that. We'll sit up in my room tonight, and wait until he passes."

And so I sat up with Sir Henry, until we heard a step in the passage. We saw Barrymore pass into the same room and crouch at the window as before. Sir Henry walked into the room and Barrymore sprang up trembling.

"What are you doing here, Barrymore?"

"Nothing, sir." His agitation was so great that he could hardly speak, and the shadows sprang up and down from the shaking of his candle.

"Come, now!" said Sir Henry, sternly. "No lies! What were you doing at that window?"

"Don't ask me, Sir Henry – don't ask me! It is not my secret and I cannot tell it."

An idea occurred to me, and I took the candle from the windowsill.

"He must have been holding it as a signal," said I. "Let us see if there is any answer."

I held it as he had done, and stared out into the darkness. And then I gave a cry of exultation, for a tiny pinpoint of yellow light glowed steadily.

"There it is!" I cried.

"Now, you rascal!" cried the baronet. "Who is your confederate and what is this conspiracy?"

The man became openly defiant. "It is my business, and not yours. I will not tell."

"Then you leave my employment in disgrace. Your family has lived with mine for over a hundred years, and here I find you deep in some dark plot against me."

"No, no, sir; no, not against you!"

It was Mrs. Barrymore, paler and more horror-struck than her husband, standing at the door.

"It is my doing, Sir Henry – all mine. John has done nothing except for my sake, and because I asked him. My unhappy brother is starving on the moor. The light is a signal that food is ready for him. His light is to show the spot to bring it to."

"Then your brother is –"

"The escaped convict, sir – Selden, the criminal."

Sir Henry and I stared at the woman in amazement. Was it possible that this respectable person was related to one of the most notorious criminals in the country?

"Yes, sir, he is my younger brother. When he dragged himself here one night, weary and starving with the warders hard at his heels, what could we do? We took him in and fed him and cared for him. Then you returned, sir, and my brother thought he would be safer on the moor until the hue and cry was over, so he lay in hiding there. But every second night we made sure he was still there by putting a light in the window. If there was an answer my husband took out some food to him. We hoped he would go, but while he was there we could not desert him."

The woman's words came with an intense earnestness which carried conviction with them.

"Well, Barrymore," said Sir Henry, "I cannot blame you for standing by your own wife. Forget what I have said. Go to your room, and we shall talk further about this matter in the morning."

When they were gone we looked out of the window again. Sir Henry had flung it open, and the cold night wind beat in upon our faces. Far away in the black distance there still glowed that one tiny point of yellow light.

"By thunder, Watson, I am going out to take that man!"

*Was it possible that this respectable person was related to one of the most notorious criminals in the country?*

In five minutes we were outside the door. Clouds were driving over the face of the sky, and just as we came out on the moor a thin rain began to fall. The light still burned steadily in front.

"What would Holmes say?" said the baronet. "How about that hour of darkness in which the power of evil is exalted?"

Suddenly out of the vast gloom of the moor arose that strange cry which I had heard on Grimpen Mire. It came through the silence of the night, a long, deep mutter, then a rising howl, and then the sad moan in which it died away. Again and again it sounded, the whole air throbbing with it. The baronet's face glimmered through the darkness.

"Good heavens, what's that, Watson?"

"I don't know. I heard it once before."

Silence closed in upon us.

"Watson," said the baronet. There was a break in his voice which told of his sudden horror. "What do folk call that sound?"

I could not escape the question. "They say it is the cry of the Hound of the Baskervilles."

He was silent for a few moments. "My God," he said at last, "can there be some truth in all these stories? Is it possible that I am really in danger? It was one thing to laugh about it in London, but another to stand out here in the darkness and to hear such a cry as that."

We stumbled along in the darkness, with the black loom of the craggy hills around us, and the yellow speck of light burning steadily in front. At last, crouching behind a granite boulder, we gazed upon a guttering candle stuck in a crevice of the rocks.

"Wait here," said I, "let us see if we can get a glimpse of him."

The words were hardly out of my mouth when we saw him. Over the rocks thrust out a terrible animal face. The light beneath him was reflected in his cunning eyes, which peered fiercely through the darkness, like a crafty animal who has heard the steps of the hunters.

Sir Henry and I sprang forward. The convict turned to run, springing over the stones like a mountain goat. We ran until we were out of breath, but the space between us grew ever wider. Finally we stopped and sat panting on two rocks.

There suddenly occurred a most strange and unexpected thing.

**The great beyond**
*Despite being the creator of the utterly rational Holmes, Conan Doyle (like many of his contemporaries) was drawn to the supernatural. He frequently attended seances, where people attempted to make contact with the souls of the dead.*

**The power of evil**
*Amulets are charms to keep evil spirits away. These Egyptian amulets come from Conan Doyle's own collection.*

The moon was low, and the jagged pinnacle of a granite tor stood up against the lower curve of its silver disc. Outlined as black as ebony on that shining background, I saw the figure of a man upon the tor. His arms were folded and his head bowed, as if he were brooding over that enormous wilderness of peat and granite which lay behind him. He might have been the spirit of that terrible place. It was not the convict, but a much taller man. With a cry of surprise I pointed at him, but in that instant the man was gone.

Extract from the Diary of Dr Watson

October 16th

This morning Barrymore said he thought it unfair on our part to hunt his brother-in-law down. "I assure you, Sir Henry, that in a few days he will be on his way to South America. I beg you not to tell the police he is still on the moor. They have given up the chase there, and he can lie quiet until a ship is ready for him."

"What if he holds someone up before he goes?" said Sir Henry.

"To commit a crime would expose where he was hiding, sir."

"True," said Sir Henry. "After what we have heard, I don't feel I could give the man up. All right, Barrymore, you can go."

"God bless you, sir, and thank you. You've been so kind to us, sir, that I should like to do my best for you in return. I know something, Sir Henry, about poor Sir Charles' death.

The baronet and I were both upon our feet.

"I know why he was at the gate at that hour. It was to meet a woman."

"How do you know this, Barrymore?"

"Your uncle had a letter in a woman's hand that morning from Coombe Tracey. A few weeks ago my wife was cleaning Sir Charles' study, and she found the remains of a letter in the grate. It said: 'Please, please, burn this letter. Be at the gate by ten o'clock. L.L.' "

"You have no idea who L.L. is?"

"No, sir. No more than you have."

*The figure of a man upon the tor.*

43

Chapter Six

# THE MAN ON THE TOR

**Remington typewriter**
*First produced in 1873,
Remington typewriters
remained the model for all
typewriters. Typing was one
of the few jobs open to a
respectable woman because it
allowed her to work at home.*

Bronze axes (c.1200 BC)

**People of the moor**
*The Beaker folk built huts on
Dartmoor between 4000 and
2500 years ago. They also
made tools from copper and
tin found there.*

October 17th

ALL DAY TODAY the rain poured down. I put on my waterproof and walked far upon the sodden moor. I was overtaken by Dr. Mortimer driving in his dog-cart, and he gave me a lift homeward. I asked him if he knew of any woman whose initials were L.L.

"There is Laura Lyons," said he. "Frankland's daughter. She married an artist named Lyons, who proved to be a blackguard and deserted her. Her father refused to have anything to do with her, because she had married without his consent. Her story got about, and several people here helped her. Stapleton did for one, and Sir Charles. I gave a trifle myself."

That evening, when Barrymore brought me my coffee into the library, I asked him if his relation had departed or was still lurking on the moor.

" I've not heard of him since I left out food for him last, and that was three days ago, sir."

"Did you see him then?"

"No, sir, but the food was gone when next I went that way."

"Then he was certainly there?"

"So you would think, sir, unless it was the other man who took it."

I stared at Barrymore. "You know there is another man, then?"

"Yes, sir. Selden told me of him, sir, at least a week ago. At first he thought that he was the police, but soon he found that he had some lay of his own. A kind of gentleman he was, as far as he could see."

"And where did he say that he lived?"

"Among the old houses on the hillside – the stone huts where the old folk used to live."

I walked over to the window and looked at the driving clouds and the tossing, windswept trees. There, in a hut upon the moor, seemed to lie the very center of the problem.

October 19th

This morning I went to Coombe Tracey to visit Mrs Laura Lyons. I entered the sitting room and a lady who was sitting before a Remington typewriter sprang up with a smile of welcome. Her face fell, however, when she saw that I was a stranger. She asked me the object of my visit.

"It is about the late Sir Charles Baskerville," said I. "You knew him, did you not?"

"I owe a great deal to his kindness. If I am able to support myself it is largely due to him."

"How did he know enough about your affairs to be able to help you?"

"Several gentleman knew my sad history and united to help me. One was Mr Stapleton, a neighbor and friend of Sir Charles. He was very kind, and told Sir Charles about my affairs."

"Did you ever write to Sir Charles asking him to meet you?" I continued.

Mrs. Lyons flushed with anger. "Certainly not."

"Not on the very day of Sir Charles' death?"

The flush faded in an instant, and a deathly face was before me.

"Yes, I did write," she cried. " I wished him to help me. I had just learned that he was going to London and might be away for months, so I asked him to meet me. You may know that I made a rash marriage and had reason to regret it. There was a prospect of my regaining my freedom if certain expenses could be met. I thought that if Sir Charles heard the story from my own lips he would help me. But I never went."

"Why?"

"I received help from another source."

"Why, then, did you not write to Sir Charles?"

"I should have done had I not seen his death in the paper the next morning."

The woman's story hung coherently together, but when I thought of her face and manner I felt that something was being held back from me.

*Her face fell when she saw that I was a stranger.*

**Urchin**
*A mischievous and raggedly dressed child was often called an "urchin". The word actually comes from the Latin for "hedgehog".*

**Hearth and home**
*Before the advent of central heating most rooms were heated by open fires.*

On my way back I saw Mr. Frankland. He was standing, gray whiskered and red faced, outside the gate of his garden.

"Good day, Dr. Watson," cried he. "You must give your horses a rest, and come in."

We went inside, and I sent Perkins and the wagonette home, sending a message to Sir Henry that I should walk over in time for dinner.

After awhile Frankland mentioned the convict on the moor.

"How do you know he is anywhere upon the moor?" said I.

"I know it because I have seen with my own eyes the messenger who takes him his food. It is taken to him by a child. I see him every day though my telescope upon the roof."

A child! Barrymore had said that our unknown was supplied by a boy. It was on his track, and not upon the convict's, that Frankland had stumbled.

"I have seen the boy again and – but wait a moment, Dr Watson! Do my eyes deceive me or is there something moving upon that hillside?"

It was several miles off, but I could distinctly see a small dark dot against the dull green and gray.

"Come, sir, come!" cried Frankland, rushing upstairs. "You will see with your own eyes and judge for yourself."

Frankland clapped his eye to the telescope and gave a cry of satisfaction. "Quick, Dr. Watson, before he passes over the hill!"

There he was, sure enough, a small urchin with a little bundle upon his shoulder, toiling slowly up the hill.

"Well! Am I right?"

"Certainly, there is a boy who seems to have some secret errand."

I left soon afterward and struck off across the moor and made for the stony hill over which the boy had disappeared.

The sun was already sinking when I reached the summit. The boy was nowhere to be seen. But down beneath me in a cleft of the hills there was a circle of the old stone huts, and in the middle of them there was one which retained sufficient roof to act as a screen against the weather. My heart leaped within me as I saw it.

This must be the burrow where the stranger lurked.

Throwing aside my cigarette, I closed my hand upon the butt of my revolver, and, walking swiftly up to the door, I looked in. The place was empty.

But this was certainly where the man lived. Some blankets rolled in a waterproof lay upon a stone slab. The ashes of a fire were heaped in a rude grate. Beside it lay some cooking utensils and a bucket half full of water. A litter of empty tins showed that the place had been occupied for some time. In the middle of the hut a flat stone served as a table, and upon this stood a small cloth bundle. My heart leaped to see that beneath it lay a sheet of paper with writing on it, and this is what I read:

*This was certainly where the man lived.*

*Dr. Watson has gone to Coombe Tracey*

Outside the sun was sinking low. All was sweet and mellow in the golden evening light, and yet my soul shared none of the peace of Nature. With tingling nerves, but a fixed purpose, I sat in the dark recess of the hut and waited for the coming of its tenant.

And then at last I heard him. Far away came the sharp clink of a boot striking upon a stone. Then another and yet another, coming nearer and nearer. I shrank back into the darkest corner, and cocked the pistol in my pocket. There was a long pause, then once more the footsteps approached and a shadow fell across the opening of the hut.

"It is a lovely evening, my dear Watson," said a well-known voice. "I really think that you will be more comfortable outside than in."

### Tinned food
*In 1809, Nicholas Appert placed cooked food in jars, sealed the tops with cork, and submerged the jars in boiling water to sterilize the food inside. A year later, tin-plated cans began to take the place of bottles.*

**Revolver**
*Watson probably owned his own revolver because he had previously served in the army. Nowadays, people must have a special permit if they want to own a gun.*

Conan Doyle had this cigarette case made for Sidney Paget, the first illustrator of the Sherlock Holmes stories.

Chapter Seven

# DEATH ON THE MOOR

I SAT BREATHLESS, hardly able to believe my ears. That cold, ironical voice could belong to but one man in all the world. "Holmes!" I cried – "Holmes!"

"Come out," said he, "and please be careful with the revolver."

He sat upon a stone, his gray eyes dancing with amusement. "I had no idea that you were inside until I was within twenty paces of the door. But if you seriously desire to deceive me you must change your tobacconist; for when I see the stub of a cigarette marked Bradley, Oxford Street, I know that my friend Watson is nearby."

"But I thought that you were in Baker Street!"

"That was what I wished you to think. Had I been with Sir Henry and you my presence would have warned our opponents to be on their guard. As it is, I have been able to get about as I could not possibly have done had I been living at the Hall. I brought the Cartwright boy down with me, and he has seen to my simple wants."

In the hut I told Holmes of my conversation with Mrs. Laura Lyons. "You realize," he said, "that a close intimacy exists between this lady and Stapleton. If I could use it to detach his wife –"

"His wife?"

"The lady who has passed here as Miss Stapleton is his wife."

"Good heavens, Holmes! Are you sure? Why the deception?"

"He saw she would be of more use as an unmarried woman."

All my unspoken instincts suddenly took shape and centered upon the naturalist. In that colorless man I seemed to see something terrible – a creature with a smiling face and a murderous heart. "It is he, then, who is our enemy – it is he who dogged us in London?"

"So I read the riddle. He forgot himself, revealing a true piece of autobiography when he first met you. He was a schoolmaster in the north of England. A little investigation showed that a school had come to grief, and the owner had disappeared with his wife. When I learned that the missing man was devoted to entomology the identification was complete."

"And where does Mrs. Laura Lyons come in?"

"Believing Stapleton an unmarried man, she counted no doubt upon becoming his wife."

"But what is the meaning of it all? What is he after?"

Holmes' voice sank. "It is murder, Watson – cold-blooded, deliberate murder. There is but one danger which can threaten us. It is that he should strike before we are ready to do so – hark!"

A terrible scream burst out of the silence of the moor that turned the blood to ice in my veins. "Oh, my God!" I gasped. "What is it?"

"The hound!" cried Holmes, "Come Watson, come! Great heavens, if we are too late!"

There came one last despairing yell, and a dull, heavy thud. And then silence.

"He has beaten us. We are too late."

"No, no, surely not!"

Blindly we ran through the gloom. At every rise Holmes looked eagerly round him, but the shadows were thick upon the moor and nothing moved on it.

A low moan fell upon our ears to our left where a ridge of rocks ended in a sheer cliff overlooking a stone-strewn slope. On its jagged face a man was spreadeagled face downward. We scrambled down the cliff, and Holmes touched the motionless figure. He struck a match and illuminated his clotted fingers and the ghastly pool which flowed from the crushed skull of the victim. It shone upon something else which turned our hearts sick and faint within us – the body of Sir Henry Baskerville!

*A man was spreadeagled
face downward.*

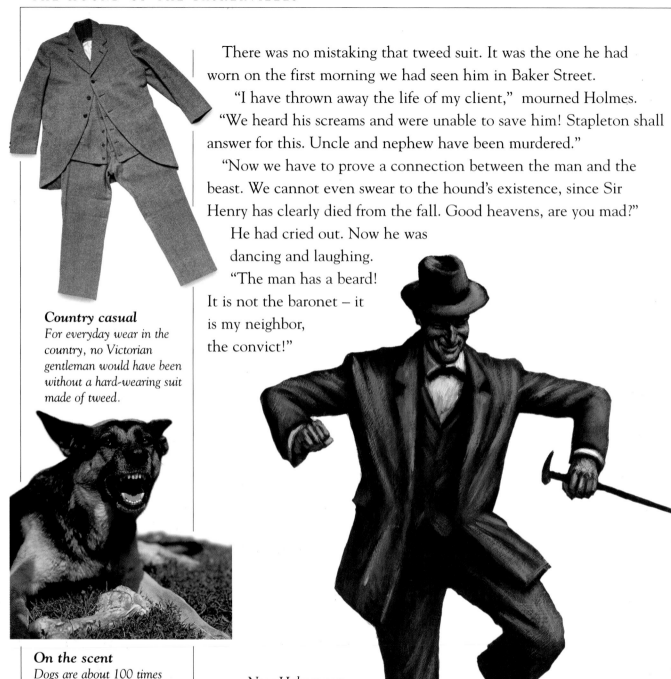

There was no mistaking that tweed suit. It was the one he had worn on the first morning we had seen him in Baker Street.

"I have thrown away the life of my client," mourned Holmes. "We heard his screams and were unable to save him! Stapleton shall answer for this. Uncle and nephew have been murdered."

"Now we have to prove a connection between the man and the beast. We cannot even swear to the hound's existence, since Sir Henry has clearly died from the fall. Good heavens, are you mad?"

He had cried out. Now he was dancing and laughing.

"The man has a beard! It is not the baronet – it is my neighbor, the convict!"

**Country casual**
*For everyday wear in the country, no Victorian gentleman would have been without a hard-wearing suit made of tweed.*

**On the scent**
*Dogs are about 100 times more receptive to smells than humans. A well-trained hound can be "laid on" by being given an article to smell. It will then hunt for other animals, people, or items with the same smell.*

*Now Holmes was dancing and laughing.*

We feverishly turned the body over. It was Selden the criminal!

Then I remembered the Baronet saying that he had handed his old clothes to Barrymore, who must have passed them to Selden.

"The clothes have been the poor fellow's death," said Holmes. "The hound has been laid on from some article of Sir Henry's – probably the boot which was taken from the hotel."

A figure was approaching us over the moor – Stapleton. He stopped when he saw us. "Dear me, what's this?" he cried. "Somebody hurt? Not – don't tell me that is our friend Sir Henry!"

He stooped over the dead man and gasped.

"Who – who's this?" he stammered.

"It is Selden, the man who escaped from Princetown."

Stapleton turned a ghastly face upon us. He looked sharply from Holmes to me. "Dear me! How did he die?"

"He appears to have broken his neck falling over these rocks. We were strolling on the moor when we heard a cry."

"Me too. I was expecting Sir Henry and became alarmed when he did not come. Did you hear anything else? They say a phantom hound is heard at night upon the moor."

"We heard nothing of the kind," said I.

"And what is your theory of this poor fellow's death?"

"Anxiety and exposure have driven him mad. He rushed about the moor in a crazy state, then fell and broke his neck."

"That seems the most reasonable theory," said Stapleton and he gave a sigh which I took to indicate his relief. "What do you think, Mr. Holmes?"

My friend bowed. "You are quick at identification," said he. "I have no doubt that my friend's explanation will cover the facts."

We decided to leave the body until the next morning.

Holmes and I set off to Baskerville Hall, leaving the naturalist to return alone.

**Civil war**
*From 1642-49, England
suffered a civil war. The
Roundhead supported
Parliament and wanted to
abolish the monarchy, and
the Cavaliers favored rule
solely by King Charles I.
The Roundheads won, but
the monarchy was later
restored.*

*The face of Stapleton had
sprung out of the canvas.*

As we reached the Baskerville gates, Holmes said,
"Say nothing of the hound to Sir Henry. Let him think that
Selden's death was as Stapleton would have us believe."

Sir Henry was pleased to see Sherlock Holmes, but first I had the
unpleasant duty of breaking the news of Selden's death to Barrymore
and his wife. To him it may have been a relief, but she wept bitterly.

We sat down to a belated supper. "How about the case?" asked the
Baronet. "Have you made anything out of the tangle?"

"I think that I shall be in a position to make the situation rather
more clear before long," replied Holmes. "But I will need your help."

"Whatever you tell me to do I will do."

"If you do this I think our little problem will soon be solved –"
He stopped suddenly and stared fixedly over my head into the air.

"What is it?" we both cried.

His eyes shone with amused exultation. "Excuse the admiration
of a connoisseur," said he, as he waved his hand toward the line of
portraits which covered the opposite wall. "This Cavalier opposite
to me – the one with the black velvet and the lace?"

"Ah, you have a right to know about him," said Sir Henry. "That
is the cause of all the mischief, the wicked Hugo, who started the
Hound of the Baskervilles."

Later, when Sir Henry had gone to his room, Holmes led me back
into the banqueting hall, his bedroom candle in his hand. He held
it up against the time-stained portrait on the wall.

"Do you see anything there?"

I looked at the broad plumed hat, the curling love-locks, the
white lace collar, and the straight severe face.

"There is something of Sir Henry about the jaw."

"Just a suggestion, perhaps. But wait an instant!"

He stood upon a chair, and holding up the light in his left hand, he curved his right arm
over the broad hat and round the long ringlets.

"Good heavens!" I cried, in amazement.

The face of Stapleton had sprung out of the canvas.

"The fellow is a Baskerville – that is evident. We have him, Watson, we have him,
and I dare swear that before tomorrow night he will be fluttering in
our net as helpless as one of his own butterflies."

**Unsigned warrant**
*Sherlock Holmes is not a police officer, so Lestrade must formally arrest the suspect for him. Lestrade is based at Scotland Yard, the home of the London Metropolitan Police, the first modern police force, which was founded in 1829.*

**Divorce**
*Now commonplace, divorce was not only a costly process, it also carried a great social stigma. Women in unhappy marriages often did not get divorced because they could not afford to support themselves.*

Next morning, Sir Henry told Holmes about his plans to visit the Stapletons that night. "I hope that you will come also."

"I fear that Watson and I must go to London."

The baronet's face perceptively lengthened.

"My dear fellow," said Holmes, "trust me. Drive to Merripit House. Then send back your trap and say you plan to walk home."

"To walk across the moor? But that is the very thing which you have so often cautioned me not to do."

"This time you may do it with safety so long as you take the straight path from Merripit House to the Grimpen Road."

We said goodbye to our friend, and a couple of hours later were at Coombe Tracey station. A boy was waiting on the platform.

"Take this train to town, Cartwright," said Holmes to the boy. "When you arrive send a wire to Sir Henry, saying that if he finds a pocket-book which I have lost he is to post it to Baker Street."

"Yes, sir."

A telegram was then handed to Holmes.

*Coming down with unsigned warrant. Arrive five-forty -*
                    LESTRADE

"This is in answer to my telegram this morning. We may need his assistance. Now, Watson, we should call upon Mrs. Laura Lyons."

Holmes opened his interview with an astonishing frankness.

"I am investigating the death of the late Sir Charles Baskerville," said he. "My friend here, Dr. Watson, has informed me of what you have communicated and withheld in this matter. You have confessed that you asked Sir Charles to be at the gate at ten o'clock. We know that was the place and hour of his death. You have withheld what the connection is between these events."

"There is no connection."

"Then the coincidence is extraordinary. But we shall establish a connection. We regard this case as murder, and the evidence may implicate not only your friend Mr. Stapleton, but his wife as well."

The lady sprang from his chair. "His wife!" she cried.

"The person who has passed for his sister is really his wife."

"Mr. Holmes, this man offered me marriage if I could divorce my husband. Now I see I was a tool in his hands. Ask me what you like.

I swear that I never dreamed any harm to the old gentleman."

"I believe you, madam," said Sherlock Holmes. "Did Stapleton suggest this letter?"

"He dictated it."

"I presume he claimed you would receive help from Sir Charles for the cost of your divorce?"

"Exactly."

"And then after you had sent the letter he dissuaded you from keeping the appointment?"

"He promised me he would devote his last penny to removing the obstacles that divided us."

"Then after Sir Charles' death he made you swear to say nothing about your appointment?"

"He said that the death was very mysterious, and I may be suspected if the facts came out."

"Quite so. But you had your suspicions?"

She hesitated and looked down.

"I think that you have had a fortunate escape," said Holmes. Good morning, Mrs Lyons."

We met Lestrade off the London train. "Anything good?" he asked.

"The biggest thing for years," said Holmes. "After dinner, we will take the London fog out of your throat by giving you a breath of the pure night air of Dartmoor."

*We met Lestrade off the London train.*

Chapter Eight

# THE HOUND OF THE BASKERVILLES

***Spooky atmosphere***
*Fog creates an air of mystery, making it indispensible to virtually every tale of the supernatural.*

*It was an enormous, coal-black hound, but not such a hound as mortal eyes have seen.*

BACK ON THE MOOR, my nerves thrilled with anticipation with every stride of the horses and turn of the wheels. We got down when we were some distance from Merripit House.

"These rocks will make an admirable screen," said Holmes. "We shall wait here. Watson, you know the lay of the land. Creep forward and see what they are doing."

I tiptoed down the path and stooped behind a low wall. I looked into the dining room where Sir Henry and Stapleton sat smoking cigars. Then Stapleton rose and left. I heard the creak of a door and the sound of boots upon gravel. He paused at the door of an outhouse. A key turned in a lock, and a scuffling noise came from within. He soon rejoined his guest. I crept back to my companions and described what I had seen.

Over Grimpen Mire hung a dense, white fog, drifting slowly in our direction. Holmes muttered, "Our success and even his life may depend upon his leaving before the fog is over the path."

The fog crawled round the house. Holmes exclaimed, "If he isn't out in a quarter of an hour the path will be covered."

As the fog-bank flowed onward we fell back until we were half a mile from the house, and still that dense white sea, with the moon silvering its upper edge, swept slowly on.

"We are too far," said Holmes. "We cannot have him overtaken before he reaches us."

Quick steps broke the silence. Through the fog stepped Sir Henry. "Hist!" cried Holmes, and I heard the sharp click of a cocking pistol. "It's coming!"

I sprang up, grasping my pistol, my mind paralyzed. It was an enormous coal-black hound, but not such a hound as mortal eyes have seen. Fire burst from its open mouth, its eyes glowed, its muzzle and hackles were outlined in flickering flame. Never in the delirious dream of a disordered brain could anything more hellish be conceived than that dark form and savage face which broke out of the wall of fog.

With long bounds the huge black creature leaped down the track, hard upon the footsteps of our friend. So paralyzed were we by the apparition that we allowed him to pass. Then Holmes and I both fired, and the creature howled. It did not pause, however, but bounded onward. Far away on the path we saw Sir Henry looking back, his face white in the moonlight, his hands raised in horror, glaring helplessly at the frightful thing hunting him down.

But that cry of pain from the hound blew all our fears to the winds. If he was vulnerable he was mortal, and we could kill him. In front of us we heard screams from Sir Henry and the deep roar of the hound. I was in time to see the beast spring upon its victim, hurl him to the ground and worry at his throat. But the next instant Holmes emptied five barrels of his revolver into the creature's flank. With a howl of agony it fell limp upon its side. The giant hound was dead.

Lestrade thrust his brandy-flask into the Baronet's mouth, and two worried eyes gazed at us.

"My God!" he whispered. "What in Heaven's name was it?"

"It's dead," said Holmes. "The family ghost is laid."

In mere size and strength it was a terrible creature which was lying stretched before us. I placed my hand upon the glowing muzzle, and as I held them up my own fingers smoldered and gleamed in the darkness.

"Phosphorus," I said.

We helped Sir Henry to a rock and left him to rest, retracing our steps swiftly down the path.

*A figure was tied, swathed and muffled in sheets.*

The front door of Merripit House was open but we could see no sign of our man. On the upper floor, however, one of the bedroom doors was locked. A faint moaning came from within. Holmes struck the door and it flew open. We all three rushed into the room.

In the center was an upright beam to which a figure was tied, swathed and muffled in sheets. We tore off the gag and unswathed the bonds. Mrs. Stapleton sank to the floor in front of us.

"Lestrade," cried Holmes, "your brandy bottle! Sit her down."

She opened her eyes. "Oh, the villain! See how he has treated me! But this is nothing! It is my mind and soul that he has tortured and defiled. I could endure it all, as long as I had his love, but now I know that in this also I have been his dupe." She broke into passionate sobbing as she spoke.

"Tell us, then, madam," said Holmes, "where we shall find him. If you have ever aided him in evil, help us now and so atone."

"There is an old tin mine in the Mire where he kept his hound. That is where he would fly."

The fog-bank lay like white wool against the window.

"No one could find his way into the Grimpen Mire tonight," said Holmes.

"He may find his way in, but never out," she cried. "How can he see the guiding wands tonight? We planted them together, he and I, to mark the pathway through the Mire."

It was evident that pursuit was in vain until the fog had lifted so we returned with the Baronet to Baskerville Hall.

The next morning the fog had vanished. Mrs. Stapleton guided us to the point where they had found a pathway through the bog. We left her standing upon the firm soil which tapered out into the bog. Small wands planted here and there showed where the path zig-zagged between tufts of rushes. A false step plunged us more than once thigh-deep into the mire.

From amid a tuft of cotton-grass some dark thing was projecting. Holmes sank to his waist as he stepped from the path to seize it and held an old black boot in the air.

"Meyers, Toronto" was printed on the leather inside.

"It is worth a mud bath," said he. "It is our friend Sir Henry's missing boot."

"Thrown there by Stapleton in his flight."

"Exactly. He retained it after using it to set the hound upon his track, then hurled it away. We know at least that he came so far in safety."

Reaching firmer ground we looked eagerly for footsteps. But none met our eyes. Somewhere in the heart of Grimpen Mire, down in the foul slime of the huge morass which had sucked him in, this cold, cruel-hearted man is forever buried.

**Luminous glow**
*Stapleton used white phosphorous to enhance the huge hound's terrifying appearance. Phosphorescent paint is also used to make the hands of clocks and watches glow in the dark.*

Chapter Nine

# A RETROSPECTION

IT WAS THE END of November, and Holmes and I sat, upon a raw and foggy night, on either side of a blazing fire in our sitting-room in Baker Street. "The whole course of events," remarked Holmes, "was simple, although to us it appeared complex."

"My inquiries show that the family portrait did not lie, and that this fellow Stapleton was indeed a Baskerville. He was a son of Rodger Baskerville, the younger brother of Sir Charles, who fled with a sinister reputation to South America where he was said to have died unmarried. He did, as a matter of fact, marry, and had one child, this fellow. He married Beryl Garcia, one of the beauties of Costa Rica, and, having purloined a considerable sum of public money, changed his name to Vandeleur, fled to England and established a school in Yorkshire. The school began well but soon sank from disrepute into infamy. The Vandeleurs changed their name to Stapleton and moved to the south of England.

"Stapleton had discovered that only two lives intervened between him and a valuable estate. He took his wife with him as his sister, and cultivated Sir Charles Baskerville's friendship. The idea of using her as a decoy was clearly in his mind. He meant to have the estate, and he was ready to use any tool or run any risk for that end.

"The baronet himself told him about the family hound, and so prepared the way for his own death. Stapleton had learned from Dr. Mortimer that the old man's heart was weak, and that a shock would kill him. He had heard also that Sir Charles was superstitious, and had taken this grim legend very seriously. His ingenious mind instantly suggested a way by which the baronet could be done to death.

"Stapleton bought a strong, savage dog. He had already on his insect hunts learned to penetrate the Grimpen Mire, and so had a safe hiding-place for the creature. He hoped that his wife might lure Sir Charles to his ruin, but she refused. Then he thought of Laura Lyons, whom he knew about through Sir Charles. By representing himself as a single man, he told her that in the event of her obtaining a divorce he would marry her. When he learned that Sir Charles was about to leave the Hall on the advice of Dr. Mortimer, he told Mrs. Lyons to write a letter, imploring the old man to meet her on the evening before his departure for London. He then prevented her from going and so had the chance for which he had waited.

"He treated his hound with his infernal paint, and brought the beast round to the gate where the old gentleman waited. The dog, incited by its master, sprang over the wicket-gate and pursued the baronet, who fled screaming down the Yew Alley.

"The hound kept upon the grassy border while the baronet ran down the path, so that no track but the man's was visible. On seeing him lying still the creature probably approached to sniff at him, but finding him dead, turned away. It was then that it left the print which was observed by Dr. Mortimer. The hound was then called away to its lair in the Grimpen Mire.

"You perceive the devilish cunning of it, for it would be almost impossible to make a case against the real murderer. His only accomplice was one who could never give him away.

"From Dr. Mortimer, Stapleton learned about the arrival of Henry Baskerville. His first idea was that Sir Henry might be done to death in London. His wife did not dare to write to warn Sir Henry. Instead, she cut out words to form a message and addressed the letter in a disguised hand. This gave the baronet his first warning of danger.

"It was essential for Stapleton to get an article of Sir Henry's clothing, so that, in case he was driven to use the dog, he might have the means of setting him upon his track. The first boot he procured was new, and useless for his purpose. He had it returned and obtained another.

"When Stapleton understood that I had taken over the case in London, he returned to Dartmoor and awaited the arrival of the baronet.

"It was my game to watch and wait. Therefore I came down secretly. Your reports reached me rapidly, being forwarded from Baker Street to Coombe Tracey, and I was able to establish the real identity of Stapleton and his wife. Yet I still did not have a case that could go to a jury. There was no alternative but to catch him red-handed, and to do so we had to use Sir Henry as bait. We succeeded at a cost which Dr. Mortimer assures me will be a temporary one. A long journey may enable our friend to recover not only from his shattered nerves but also from his wounded feelings. His love for Mrs. Stapleton was deep.

"There can be no doubt that, although Stapleton exercised an influence over her, she was ready to warn Sir Henry so far as she could without implicating her husband. Stapleton himself was a jealous, violent man, for when he saw the baronet paying court to the lady, even though it was part of his own plan, he could not help interrupting with a passionate outburst which revealed the fiery soul which his self-contained manner concealed. By encouraging the intimacy he made it certain that Sir Henry would frequently come to Merripit House. On the day Sir Henry was to be murdered, however, his wife turned against him. A furious scene followed and he saw that she would betray him. He tied her up, therefore, that she might have no chance of warning Sir Henry.

"When Stapleton came into the succession, he probably planned to claim the property from South America, and so obtain the fortune without ever coming back to England.

"And now, my dear Watson, I think, we may turn our thoughts into more pleasant channels. I have a box for *Les Huguenots*. Might I trouble you to be ready in half an hour, and we can stop at Marcini's for a little dinner on the way?"

# CONAN DOYLE & SHERLOCK HOLMES

Conan Doyle's life was no less interesting than the stories he wrote. He studied medicine and spent seven months on board an Arctic whaling ship as a doctor. He went as a volunteer to Africa during the Boer War. He was a keen sportsman and an accomplished skier who anticipated the appeal of the sport well before it became popular. He also traveled extensively, giving lectures all over the English-speaking world. It remained a source of frustration that the public identified him so closely with Sherlock Holmes that they paid much less attention to his many other works and interests.

### Man of letters
Alongside his 60 Sherlock Holmes stories, Conan Doyle wrote science fiction, historical novels, political pamphlets, and frequent letters to the press on everything from military strategy to spiritualism.

### Sherlockiana
Today the character of Sherlock Holmes is instantly recognizable even to people who have never read the stories. There are clubs all over the world dedicated to Holmes as well as Sherlockian scholars and collectors.

*Articles that belonged to Sir Arthur Conan Doyle.*

### A believer in fairies
Sherlock Holmes is famous for being very rational. Yet Conan Doyle was very deeply committed to spiritualism and believed in the supernatural. He was convinced that photographs of fairies produced by two girls named Elsie Wright and Frances Griffiths were genuine. However, 70 years later, Elsie

*The Sherlock Holmes stories were first published in The Strand Magazine.*

*An early American edition of The Hound of the Baskervilles.*

### Holmes' study
The 1951 Festival of Britain featured a Sherlock Holmes exhibition that traveled the world. In 1957, a superb reconstruction of the great detective's study found a permanent home in The Sherlock Holmes pub in London.

*One of many movies based on the book, this version was produced by Hammer in 1959.*

## HOLMES ON STAGE AND SCREEN

*William Gillette played the detective on stage with the author's approval for over 30 years beginning in 1916. Since then, every generation has created the character anew.*

### Young Sherlock Holmes
This Paramount film featuring Nicholas Rowe and Alan Cox was made in 1985.

### Star of the silver screen
In the 1940s, Basil Rathbone (below) epitomized Holmes. He played the detective in 14 films between 1939-46.

### A hundred years of Holmes
Granada TV produced five series of programs starring Jeremy Brett as Holmes and Edward Hardwicke at Dr. Watson between 1984–93. These have been screened in over 70 countries.

SIR ARTHUR CONAN DOYLE'S
THE HOUND OF THE BASKERVILLES
WITH RICHARD GREENE BASIL RATHBONE WENDY BARRIE
AND NIGEL BRUCE LIONEL ATWILL
JOHN CARRADINE BARLOWE BORLAND
BERYL MERCER MORTON LOWRY RALPH FORBES
DARRYL F. ZANUCK IN CHARGE OF PRODUCTION
A 20TH CENTURY-FOX PICTURE
DIRECTED BY SIDNEY LANFIELD ASSOCIATE PRODUCER GENE MARKEY SCREEN PLAY BY ERNEST PASCAL

*Joan Hickson as Miss Marple*

### Super sleuths
Crime writer Agatha Christie created two famous detectives – Miss Marple and Hercule Poirot.

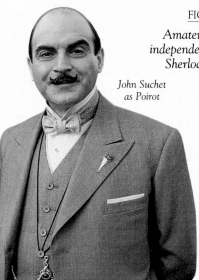

*John Suchet as Poirot*

## FICTIONAL DETECTIVES

*Amateur detectives, often working independently from the police – just like Sherlock Holmes – are a staple of modern TV drama.*

### The X Files
In the 1990s, *The X Files* captured the popular imagination. Mulder and Scully's caseload involved both science and the supernatural. Conan Doyle would have approved – he believed in the paranormal and also wrote science fiction himself.

# Acknowledgments

**Picture Credits**
The publishers would like to thank
the following for their kind permission
to reproduce the photographs.

Picture credits:
(t = top, b = bottom, l = left, r = right, c =
center, a = above)

AKG (London): 6c, 30tl, 34tl, 44bl, 56tl,

The Art Archive: 18bl,

Nathan L Bengis *Holmes with Pipe*: 6bl,

Bridgeman Art Library: 5, 8tl, 20tl, 23tr,
38cl, 46bl, 48t, 54bl, 62bl,

Bruce Coleman Collection: 15tr, 32-3
(butterflies), 50bl,

Mary Evans Picture Library: 6tr, 7c, 25cr,
28cl, 32tl, 36b, 37tr, 38tl, 46tl, 47br, 52tl,
62tl, tr,

Granada Television: 63tl,

Ronald Grant Archive: 40, 63tr, cr, bl, br
(9852) *David Suchet as Poirot* 63bc,

C 1959, 1996 Hammer Film Productions
Ltd *Postcard advertising Hammer
Production of Hound of the Baskervilles*
62br,

Robert Harding Picture Library: Nigel
Francis (505/2449) security camera 7br,
(612/492) clock: 59tr,

Hulton Getty Picture Collection: 6cl, 42t,
54tl,

Liz Moore: 7cr,

Science & Society Picture Library: 25br,
44tl,

Science Photo Library: 7tl, tr,

Additional photography by: Frank
Greenaway, Bob Langrish, Andy Crawford.

Thanks particularly to Richard Lancelyn Green for
Sir Arthur Conan Doyle artefacts;  also to James
Smith & Sons (Umbrellas) Ltd for loan of a Penang
Lawyer; Grock Lockhart for editorial assistance.